UNDER THE WORLD

UNDER THE WORLD

E. CHRISTOPHER CLARK

CLARKWOODS
BOOKS

Published in the United States by Clarkwoods in Chelmsford, Massachusetts.

ISBN for the Print Edition: 978-1-952044-19-9
ISBN for the Digital Edition: 978-1-952044-18-2

Library of Congress Control Number: 2020904427

CONTENTS

For my Genre Fiction students from the Fall of 2016, without whom I wouldn't have made it through that dark season

THE PIECES

When I see you again, for the first time in months, I'm surfing the waves of the Red Line. Feet planted, hands in my pockets, I refuse to reach for the train's handrail to keep my balance. I *refuse*, just flat-out won't do it— even when the vision of you threatens to sweep the legs out from under me like you're Johnny and I'm the Karate Kid.

It can't be you, I think to myself, not with that smile. No one smiles like that. No. Not after God gives you more than you can handle and only a surgical oncologist can take the weight off your shoulders. (Or your breasts, as the case may be.)

It can't be you. But it *is* you.

Those are *your* keys twirling around that finger that must be yours as well. And that's *your* knee pressed up against that old codger's thigh. And those are your eyes staring at him—rapt, as he raps to you about a dream he had last night. I'm rapt, too. It's only when he stops speaking to wiggle a tooth that I look away.

And that's when I spot the green lipstick stain on his collar. The stain *you* must have left there, because that's the shade—the *chartreuse*—that I ran down to the Dollar Tree to buy for you last Halloween. You were going as Poison Ivy to my Penguin, and nothing you had in your makeup case was gaudy enough. And even though I offered to go to a real store, with a real selection, you were like "No." Trash was what you were going for, so trash was what you were going to get.

Or what I was going to get for you, I guess.

I wonder if the codger you've been kissing runs errands for you now, or if he's just another fling—just another wild oat you're looking to sow before you're sown into the earth yourself.

In my mind, I see the two of you in bed together, your ripe body wrapped around his withered one. And then I see myself, reflected in the darkened window of the train's closed doors. I'm in the suit that's my uniform once again, rather than the flannel and jeans you dressed me in each morning of my unemployment —the costume you cobbled together to make me look like the kid you knew back in the day, the one who still had something to offer the world. Even if it had been twenty years since I did.

Your old man's dream is about teeth, I finally discern, after he stops wiggling and gets back to wittering.

I bare my teeth at my reflection, feign a scream to complete the image, and read the words on the chapped lips your kissing these days:

Mentally emaciated, he says.

Mentally *emaciated.*

I'm emaciated just thinking about this. But only mentally, of course. I've still got the paunch you swore was the best pillow upon which you'd ever lain your weary head. I've still got the dad bod that's supposed to be *en vogue* these days—even though the last lady I hit on told me I was never gonna get it. Never. Gonna. Get it.

The train stops, and I follow an elderly couple out onto the platform, daydreaming all the while. I dream of your fingers plugged into holes where my teeth should be, of a village without pavement from one of the books my dentist kept in his waiting room when I was a kid, and of the tunnels you used to dream of all the damn time. Back when you were the dreamer, and I was the one who listened. And it was my knee pressed against your thigh.

But now the train is leaving, and I bring myself back to reality to watch it go.

And here's the thing: it's empty.

Where did you go? I wonder. Then I look around the platform, and I can't remember where I am. I can't remember where I'm supposed to be.

Maybe it's not you whose gone missing. Maybe it's me.

HOUSE OF THRONES, GAME OF CARDS

Nasha stood at edge of the loading dock, a pocket watch in their hand and a scowl on their face. They stared across the alley at the nothing that ringed the house and waited for the veil of the world to be drawn back one last time. Behind them, heels clicked and clacked against the hard wood of the hallway, but even as the person wearing them drew closer, Nasha made no move for the sword hanging on their left hip, nor for the gun strapped to their right. It wasn't until a hand wrapped round the back of their neck that Nasha flinched.

"Late?" asked Inda as she pushed her fingers into Nasha's hair.

Nasha said nothing.

"We could start without them," said Inda, stroking the smooth skin behind Nasha's ear.

Nasha turned to face Inda then, gave the damnable woman a scowl.

Inda pinched Nasha's earlobe between her thumb and forefinger, then gave Nasha a wicked smile. Tugging at the ear, Inda said, "My little stickler." Then she let go and sauntered across the dock, finally giving Nasha the space they knew well enough not to ask for out loud.

Inda waved a hand at the nothing. "How long has it been black now? Since the last game?"

Nasha nodded.

Inda rolled her eyes and sighed a heavy sigh. "You don't get sick of it?"

Nasha said nothing. The truth was that the black was easier to look at than any other color Inda had ever chosen. In the blackness, anything was possible. Anything imaginable.

Inda waved a hand and the nothing went orange. "Better?" she asked.

Orange reminded Nasha of the groves back home, the fruits of their mother's labors stretched out behind the castle's walls. It had been years since they'd seen home, since they'd laid beneath the trees with some girl they'd stolen from the market, or some boy, and made love with the smell of citrus in their nose. It had been ages since Nasha had seen the look of gratitude in a lover's eyes, the look and the tears as they swallowed air that wasn't festering and rank, as they felt hands upon them without callouses, without sores.

Inda waved another hand, sighed another sigh, and the nothing was black again. She was just about to quit the dock for the hallway when the veil of the world finally pulled back and two people appeared there in the alley, a desert stretched out behind them. One was resplendent in sea-green robes, a jeweled turban upon their head. They offered up their teeth and their bright eyes by way of apology, bowing to Inda as she descended the stairs to meet them. Nasha's attention, however, was on the other person, the hunched one with a throne of ivory and gold strapped to their back.

Nasha leapt from the dock to unburden the second person, watching as the veil drew closed behind them. Nasha pulled their sword from its scabbard and cut the ropes that bound the chair to the person's back. It crashed unceremoniously onto the cobbled stone of the alley as the person rose to their full height and thanked Nasha for their assistance.

"Careful!" said the person in the turban, stroking their long beard. "My family has sat upon that throne for a thousand generations."

"Then you should know, sir," said Inda, "that we do not tolerate lateness."

"Yes," he said, bowing his head again to her. "And we would have been quite on time," he continued, "if the gentleman had simply ceased his arguments with his sovereign."

"There are rules!" shouted the person who had carried the throne.

"Yes, yes," said the man in the turban, "but—"

But whatever words were left on his tongue, Nasha didn't need to hear them. They grabbed hold of him by the scruff of his neck and drew their blade across his throat. And only then, as the turbaned man's eyes widened in shock, as his hands flew to his throat, clutching at it as blood poured through his fingers, only then did Nasha speak.

"You carry your own throne," they said. And then they kicked the turbaned man backward, into the nothing.

✦

INSIDE THE HOUSE, around a granite table cut into a circle, Inda introduced the game's final player to the rest. "Your royal highnesses," said Inda, "please welcome the seventh member of our fellowship."

Nasha ushered in the person who'd carried the ivory throne and pointed at the empty spot at the table, directly to the left of the only empty chair. There was a stirring amongst the people already gathered and seated, for this was not the face they were expecting. But when they looked at Inda for some sense of reassurance—some manner of clarification—when they looked and were offered nothing, they said nothing in return.

"And playing on behalf of the house," said Inda, "for the fourth year running, Her Royal Highness, the Princess Nasha of Onterey."

Nasha did not wince at the pronoun as they took their seat. Back home, there was tolerance for much, but the rule of matrilineal primogeniture set down by their great grandmother remained unbroken. And there was a sister lurking in the shadows, waiting to ensure the rule remained in place if Nasha so much as breathed a word publicly about their preferences. So, while prudence dictated it, they would play the part of she. But they didn't have to like it. And they did not.

Inda strolled across the room to the cabinet that stood behind the throne of Nasha's mother. Nasha watched the woman unlock it with a key she wore round her neck, ignoring their mother as she tried to make eye contact. They watched Inda instead, trying to see which deck she might pull from the darkness, trying to gain the upper hand in some way, trying as they had for four long years. Inda, sensing this, glanced over her shoulder and offered Nasha a smile. Then she took a quick gander at the seventh player, as if trying to size them up.

"The game," said Inda, as she withdrew a new deck from the cabinet and turned to face them, "is five-card draw."

Half the old hands at the table nodded, understanding that this announcement was for the benefit of the new player. The other half rolled their ancient eyes.

"As always," said Inda, removing the cellophane from the deck, "the house will not fold." She smiled at Nasha, crinkling the cellophane in her hand until she saw Nasha grit their teeth at the sound. "Those who fold before the showdown will be allowed to leave with the seats of power they carried in."

"And if we stay until the end?" asked the seventh player.

Inda laughed. "You seemed quite familiar with the rules

outside," she said. "Have you honestly no knowledge of how the endgame plays out?"

The seventh player looked down at their hands for a moment. Nasha looked, too. The hands were scarred and calloused, the hands of a craftsperson. How the player had learned the rule about the burden of the throne remained a mystery; that knowledge was usually kept secret from the masses. But, whatever the source of their knowledge, the seventh player seemed ignorant of the rest.

"My master told me that no one ever stays until the end."

Inda laughed once more, ruffling the silver hair of Nasha's mother as she did. "Oh, some stay," she said. "And, if they do, they forfeit their thrones as recompense for the slight."

"Or," said Nasha's mother, "something far more precious."

Now it was Nasha's turn to roll their eyes, which they did as they slouched into their chair, threw back their head in exasperation, and sighed the heaviest of sigh of the evening.

"But," said the seventh player, "what if one of us wins?"

Nasha sat up straight at this, for they would not miss the chance to examine the look upon Inda's face as she addressed this query—this question that hadn't been asked once in the four years that Nasha had been playing on behalf of the house. Nasha knew the answer, but they had only ever heard Inda give it at the end of long night at the bar in the basement.

Inda narrowed her eyes as she circled the table, keeping her gaze locked on the seventh player as she made her way to them. Then, when she had drawn up alongside them, when still the player would not avert their eyes and withdraw their question, then Inda crouched until her face was level with the player's. And she hissed at them, "You will not win." Then she smiled, rose once again to her full height, and handed the deck to Nasha.

"But what if I do?" asked the seventh player.

Inda would not answer. She stalked off to the darkest corner of the room and took her seat there in the shadows.

"Are we not owed an answer?" asked the seventh player, looking about the table while Nasha shuffled.

Across the table, Nasha's mother said, "Excuse me, Mister—"

Out of the corner of their eye, Nasha watched for a wince, watched for any sign that their mother's presumption had been in error, but saw none.

"Mister Upar," he said.

"Mister Upar," said Nasha's mother. "I hope you will forgive the—"

Inda grunted in the corner. "Forgive a deity?" she spat.

Nasha's mother smiled kindly. "I hope you will forgive the reticence of our Lord and Savior, the one true Goddess, Inda of the Mount, because you see, the last person to win the game—"

"Was Inda herself," said Mister Upar, finishing the thought, his gaze fixed on the shadows. "Most interesting," he said. "Most interesting indeed."

"Shall we play?" said Nasha, glancing around the table, waiting for a nod from each of them before moving on to the next.

They dealt the cards fast and furious, each one hurtling across the table to its owner. And when the dealing was done, Nasha was the first to pick up their hand. Everyone else waited for them, as was the custom.

Nasha examined their cards and found the hand strong, but before they decided what they might discard, or whether they would discard at all, they took a quick look around the table.

Nergard was running a hand through the wild tangle of red locks upon his head, stewing as he always did at the start of the game. Srima sat stoic in her kimono, still staring at the cards, not yet daring to pick them up. Merama had already folded and had turned her painted face to Roway, the Crowned Jester, who seemed to be torn between continuing to play and flirting with the other woman. Gentleman Tyon had already selected two cards to discard and was tapping them against the table. Upar held his cards close to his face, all but his eyebrows obscured.

And Nasha's mother, Queen Yona herself, was staring across the table at her child, trying once again to understand the flesh of her flesh. Trying and, judging by the way she was frowning, failing.

Nasha looked at their hand again, studied the sidelong glances of the three kings they found there, and wondered what to do with the ten and the nine that stood beside them. They wished that the whole room did not wait on them, the whole world. They wished that someone at this table might be bold enough to prove a match for them, but they also knew all too well the price of hubris in the House of Thrones.

"Mister Upar," said Nasha, "the house defers. You may begin the draw."

Upar nodded, examined his hand one last time, then pushed a single card toward Nasha. Nasha dealt him a new card and wondered at his gambit. Did he have the cards to beat them? And did he have the stones to try?

This was the question. It might also be the answer.

As Nasha dealt cards to the others—three to Nergard, two each to Srima, Tyon, Roway, and their mother—they considered what might happen if they let Upar win. Nasha knew each of the others all too well to hand Inda's house keys to them, knew all too well the iniquities of these selfish fools, knew all too well the tyranny of evil men. And women, they thought, looking for once into the withered face of their mother, staring deep into her now-watering gray eyes. All they knew of Upar was his respect for the rules of the game. Perhaps he would be a just god. There was a chance of it. And was there any real chance that he would be worse than Inda?

"Nasha?" said their mother. "The table waits for you."

There was a creaking in the shadows, the sound of a chair being vacated, and then Inda stepped out of the darkness.

Nasha watched as Inda rounded the table, closed their eyes as they felt the goddess' hands squeeze their shoulders, flinched as hot breath across the nape of their neck presaged a whisper in their ear.

"What are you thinking?" hissed Inda.

Nasha tried to wipe clean the slate of their mind, fearful of what Inda might do with what she found there, but they were not quick enough.

What if he loses? asked the voice of Inda inside Nasha's head. *What if you hand everything to one of the others?*

None of them will play through to the end, thought Nasha.

If they see you lay down four cards, they might.

Nasha turned their head to look at Inda. Thoughts were one thing, not much more useful than words. The look in a person's eyes, however...

I can give you what you want, thought Inda, smiling.

How? thought Nasha.

Inda smiled and nodded at Nasha's mother. *We can both have what we want, my bold princess. Stand pat, win the game, and your mother's seat is yours.*

On the day Nasha's mother lost the game four years before, the veil had been lifted from the shadows lurking at the foot of Nasha's bed. Face nuzzled between the breasts of the village girl they brought into the palace proper each time their mother absconded for her ritual, Nasha stirred slowly. In fact, it wasn't the sound of their name that woke them at all—it was the chill creeping from the alley on the other side of the veil; they heard their name only the third time their mother spoke it, only when the two syllables were cleaved from each other by a choked-back sob.

Their mother could not look at their naked body as she told them to get dressed, to come as quickly as they could. Their mother could not look at them as they asked why, as they asked if this were a dream or if that really was the House of Thrones standing behind her. Their mother could not look at this body that had so delighted her in its infancy, in its juvenescence, this body that she had carved from her own and breathed life into. She couldn't look, and she couldn't even speak, at least not more than one word at a time. "Quickly," she said. "Quickly."

When they were a child, their mother brought them to bed with her to keep the bed warm and the nightmares at bay. When their mother shook in the night, it was Nasha's job to judge the severity, and to wake her if necessary. And so, holding a hand to their mother's quivering body, counting the shudders of its protest against the tricks the mind was playing against it, Nasha spent many a sleepless night wondering what would happen if they simply let their mother quake against them through the night, if they let her body sort itself out. What would happen if they grew numb to the violence raging beside them, if they slept on when their mother needed them most?

It was this tableau, of waking up beside the cooling husk of a now still body—it was *this* that took hold of Nasha's imagination as Inda made her suggestion. Not some garish spectacle wrought by the poisoned cup that Inda held forth at the edge of Nasha's mind's eye, nor a pageant of gore made possible by the sword hanging heavy on Nasha's hip. It was this image of their mother's demise that confronted them as they held their cards before them, as the eyes of every person at the table focused on them.

"Nasha," said their mother again. "What's your play?"

Nasha laid one card down upon the discard pile. Then another. Then two more.

Inda rose to her full height and stalked away, her heels clicking menacingly as she circled the table to stand behind Nasha's mother. Nasha looked at the angry goddess for a moment, trying to read the blank look upon her face, then got back to the task at hand.

The first card they drew was a Jack of Hearts, the second its queen, the third its king. When Nasha looked up in between the third and fourth cards, Inda was smiling.

The fourth card was, of course, the Ace. And the card they'd kept—they blinked, then checked again just to be sure—was the Ten.

The faces around the table were stunned by how much Nasha had laid down, wondering at what they'd received in return. Their eyes were wide, their eyebrows raised, and their jaws agape— except for Roway, who wore a devilish grin now, and seemed to be on the verge of laughing with delight. Presently, the players hid themselves back behind their cards, trying to make their decisions.

But Nasha wanted it over with, so they delivered the one line they had left to give in this absolute farce: "Does anyone fold?"

Nergard, with an exasperated grunt, laid his cards down and pushed them away from himself. Srima closed her eyes whilst she ran her free hand back and forth along the pearl-encrusted arm of her throne, then she folded too. Tyon and Roway exchanged glances, as if each was trying to see if the other was bold enough to take the risk. There was a great deal of squinting and several tilts of each head before they nodded and laid their cards down, leaning back into their chairs to see what happened next.

That left Nasha's mother and Upar. Nasha gave Upar a side-long glance and found him just as stone-faced as he had been for most of the game. So they turned their attention to their mother, whose chest and shoulders heaved with each deep breath she took.

"Yona," said Inda as she massaged the shoulders of Nasha's mother. "Do you fold?"

Nasha's mother breathed in deep one last time, then shook her head in a silent "no." She could not see the smile worn now by the woman standing behind her.

"Lay down your cards then," said Inda.

Nasha's mother fanned her hand upon the table, revealing four Nines and the Four of Hearts. Upar laid down one card at a time, beginning with the One of Clubs, then the two, his smile broadening with each reveal until his skin was as flush as the hand he'd been dealt.

They looked to Nasha then, everyone waiting to see what cards fate had seen fit to grant their host. And though Nasha did not want to see what was about to happen, they knew there was no sense in prolonging the inevitable. They laid their cards down.

There was an uproar as Upar's head hung low, as Queen Yona sobbed. "How?" asked Tyon as Nergard bellowed the word "LIES" in every tongue he could muster. Roway laughed maniacally. Srima sat silent as Merama muttered, "Such luck has never before been seen in these hallowed halls."

Nasha felt a hand on their arm, a gentle squeeze. They turned to face Upar as he asked, "What happens now?"

"You go home," said Nasha. "Your throne stays here."

"But who will rule?" said Upar.

Nasha nodded at Inda and said nothing more.

"And what of your kingdom?" said Upar. "Will it be the same there, now that your mother has lost for a second time?"

"Oh no," said Inda from across the room and above the din. "There is much hubris in the hills of Onterey," she said, the room quieting around her as she moved her hands from the shoulders of Nasha's mother to top of her throne. "One cannot rule such a proud people from afar," said Inda. "I will need a regent, of course."

"But who?" said Nergard, waving a hand at Nasha's mother. "Do you mean to go easy on this vain wench once again?"

"Oh no," said Inda. And then, with a smile on her face, she yanked the throne backwards.

Nasha's mother toppled to the floor, but no one came to her aid. They sat silent and still now, the whole lot of them, waiting to see what Inda would do next.

And what she did next was this: Inda raised her leg as high as her skirt would allow, then stomped her heel down upon the back of the old queen's neck.

The room kept quiet in spite of the horror playing out before them, silent except for a choking sound that ended only with the squelch of heel withdrawing from flesh. Then Inda said, in a calm, cold voice, "Leave," and all but Nasha did as they were told.

Nasha rounded the table and stood above their mother's lifeless body for a moment, taking in what a dream made reality looked like. Then they fell to their knees and cradled the head of their mother's corpse in their lap.

"You will return to your kingdom," said Inda, stalking away, leaving a trail of bloody heel prints on the stone floor behind her. "You will rule in my stead, but as you see fit."

"And what of the game?" asked Nasha.

Inda sat upon the far end of the table, wiping the blood from her shoe with one bent card after another. Distracted, she said nothing.

"What of the game?" shouted Nasha, ashamed of the sob that choked their voice.

Inda smiled. "You will return each time I call for you," she said. "And you will play for the house as you have these four years. For there has never been a more shrewd gamesman than you, my dear. No one has ever played the game as well," she said.

Except me, she thought, loud enough that Nasha could hear her above the cacophony of memories—memories of orange groves, and warm beds, and a heart that loved them the only way it knew how.

TIME'S FOOL

The halfway point is where she found her brother in the ditch all those years ago—his body twisted, his chest caved in where the truck had hit him. Only half of him was mangled, but it was the wrong half, so their mother kept the casket closed anyway.

When she turns here for the jog home, Lauren doesn't stop moving, but she can't resist a moment to stare. Some mornings she shifts her weight back and forth from one leg to the other. Other days she stretches, standing on one foot then the other, bending the free leg at the knee and holding it behind her by the ankle. She might even run in place a few seconds, but she never lets herself go still.

When she looks at the leaves gathered there this morning, at the frost weighing them down, she imagines his cheek pressed against them: his warm flesh driving out the cold, bequeathing what life he had left to something already dead. Her mother called her morbid for thinking such things, but her mother had never had to see them. It had been Lauren who found Sammy there by the side of the road; Mom hadn't looked upon the corpse until the moment at the funeral home when there were decisions to be made. And at that point, after not much more than a fleeting glance, she had left the room and left the rest to her daughter.

Lauren turns and starts back toward home.

All her life she has lived in this town, minus the few years she spent tending to a marriage that never took root, and so the glistening pond nestled amongst the trees to her left is no balm for frayed nerves. The pasture to her right and the cattle grazing there, they are no reminder of a simpler age. And the horse paddocks, where she once watched her friends drive those animals over hurdle after hurdle, they offer no inspiration. She can't remember what they looked like when they leapt, can't imagine the wind in their manes and the look in their eyes as they dared to fly; all she can see now are the fences that kept them where they were, forever keep them where they are.

"If you hate it so much," Mom keeps telling her, "then why don't you leave?"

Lauren raises her wrist toward her face and the screen on her watch lights up to tell her how hard her heart is beating. She knows, of course—she can feel it—but she doesn't trust herself. She knows she's not as impartial as the sensor pressed against her skin.

As she crests the last of the modest hills on her route, the house looms large before her. Mom is on the porch in her rocking chair, an afghan laid across her lap, looking ten years older than she is. Ten years at least.

When she reaches the front steps, Lauren holds onto the handrail and doubles over. Checking her watch, she realizes she's attacked the second half of her run with a bit too much vigor and perhaps too much vim; she made great time, but she wasn't ready. Tomorrow, she realizes, sucking air through her nose and nearly choking on it, she may need to take the day off.

On the porch, Mom scoffs, mumbling something about the

path out back, the bike trail the town has paved atop its old train tracks.

"Too flat," she tells her mother, still panting, though strong enough to stand upright now. "Not enough of a challenge."

Mom shakes her head as Lauren mounts the steps. "Breathing is a challenge," she says. "That's not enough for you?"

⚜

MOM SITS OUTSIDE while Lauren is making breakfast, and though Lauren can see her shuddering harder every time she takes a peek through the kitchen window, though she wanted to tell her mother "You'll catch your death of cold" when the old woman insisted staying out for a few minutes more, she doesn't say anything. Lauren knows well enough to pick her battles.

At the kitchen table, over eggs and Canadian bacon, Mom wonders about pancakes. "Did I never teach you how to make them?" she asks.

"Reunion's on Saturday night," Lauren tells her. "I need to fit into my dress."

"Fit schmit," says Mom. "You could wear a potato sack and you'd still be the one to go home with."

"Mom," says Lauren, rolling her eyes. "It's been twenty years. Most of the people there went home with someone ages ago. And certainly those worth—"

"Picky," says Mom, cutting her off. "Always picky."

"Not always," says Lauren, rubbing her thumb along the underside of her ring finger, an old habit that's dying hard.

⚜

THE TRUCK HIT Sammy the day before Lauren's prom. There'd been a small fire at the school, the pungent stink of rubber filling the halls, and everyone was dismissed. Sammy caught a ride to a buddy's house for a few hands of Magic cards, but a few hands turned into staying for dinner and an angry phone call from Mom and the decision that Sammy, the "most inconsiderate son in the world," would walk home when he was done.

Lauren was sitting in her room that night when her mother knocked on her door. She was in her underwear, at the foot of her bed, staring at the dress hanging in her closet, at the zipper in particular. When her mother knocked a second time, Lauren had to brush a tear away before she could manage the words "Come in."

Mom opened the door and had begun to speak before she noticed the state of Lauren. She averted her eyes and said, "You could've taken a moment to get dressed."

"It sounded urgent," said Lauren, looking down now at her stomach, at her thighs, searching for something to blame.

"Your brother's not home yet," said Mom.

"You did yell wicked loud," said Lauren, standing up and crossing to her dresser, knowing already what was going to be asked of her.

"Could you go out and see if you can track him down?"

Lauren pulled open her drawer of t-shirts. "Where was he at?"

"Kevin's," said Mom. "Just down 27."

"Okay," said Lauren, pulling on the baggy Incesticide shirt her boyfriend had left the last time he'd snuck in.

"It's just that I don't think he'd take a ride from me right now."

"I'll find him," said Lauren, stepping into a pair of sweats.

And find him she did. She found him then like she finds the dress now: in the dark, forgotten and cast aside.

She pulls the dress from the back of the closet and into the light, surprised she remembered to put it back in its bag way back when. The funeral was one day, graduation the next, and her break-up the day after that. The guy said he understood why she'd bailed on prom, and maybe he did, but he said it with a hunger in his eyes. A hunger to heal her maybe, but a hunger nevertheless, and she couldn't stand to be looked at like that. She couldn't stand to think of her pain as something to be devoured, to imagine him chewing away at her anguish until he found something worth saving at the center.

Mom is knocking again. Lauren invites her in.

Mom asks: "You're going to wear that?"

"I thought it would be funny," says Lauren.

"You're trying to be funny?" says Mom, shaking her head. "I thought you were trying to get laid."

"Mom!"

Mom shudders for a moment, and Lauren extends a hand to steady her, but she just shoos Lauren off. She grabs hold of the door knob and closes her eyes until she's still.

"Mom?"

The old woman opens her eyes and forces a smile. "I can be at Elaine's," she says, "if you'd like the house to yourself."

"Mom," says Lauren, "that's not why I'm—"

"It should be," says Mom as she turns on the spot and starts back down the hall, her hand on the chair rail the whole way.

☙❧

WHEN SHE PULLS into the restaurant's parking lot, the party is already in full swing. The smokers have congregated around the side of the building, in front of the plate glass window for some shop that has its lights off—a dry cleaner maybe, but she doesn't get close enough to check—and a few of them offer waves and smiles; one shouts "Hey!" but stops short when he can't remember her name.

Inside, the bar is surrounded by kids she's known since she was five, but who she hasn't seen, for the most part, since they were throwing their tasseled caps into the air. They're exchanging tiny paper tickets with the harried bartenders, the kind they used to sell at football games to raffle off VCRs and CD boxed sets. It occurs to Lauren that she's paid in advance for a couple of these herself, and that she should probably drink before she goes any further.

The man with the wheel of tickets was their class president, and time has treated him well. The gray that flecks his hair now serves only to bolster the air of confidence he scarfed about him in those days gone by. He greets her with a warm smile and a hug, her name ready on his lips from the moment he saw her across the room. Every name seems to be ready on his lips, she realizes as she takes her tickets and makes way for the next in line, but that doesn't diminish her affection for him in this moment; it simply confirms that they all made at least one sane decision in high school. This guy was the only one for this job; she can't even remember his name, for Christ's sake, and she was *just* staring at the tag stuck to his still impressive pecs.

A whiskey sour in each hand, Lauren makes her way into the back room where most of the commotion seems to be centered. There are hors d'oeuvres on tables pushed against the walls, a small cart of booze manned by a perky blonde who's being ogled by grown men in backwards ball caps, and cluster upon cluster of classmates. Some have sequestered themselves amongst the same cliques they called home in the days of yore, but others have broken ranks. There's a cheerleader chatting up a kid who never left the art room, there's a dude who spent half of senior year doing time in detention spinning a yarn for the kid he pantsed relentlessly in the sixth grade.

"Ren's not time's fool," says a guy she once had English with, "though rosy lips and cheeks within his bending sickle's compass come."

Lauren hugs him, kisses him on the cheek, asks, "Does Shakespeare get you much play, Ian?"

He laughs. "Not with the women who can spot it."

They chat for a while, as Lauren finishes her first drink and then her second, about everything from that one time Lauren did theater with Ian ("The children's play!" she says, wondering what it was that year; "Hansel & Gretel," he tells her), everything from that to who's died from their class and when.

Morbid, she thinks, her mother's words in her ears.

"Was Robin Gates our year?" she asks Ian, pretty sure Robin wasn't, but not ready to let the conversation go. She's looked around the room a half-dozen times by now, and she's spotted no one else worth talking to. She's also pretty sure she's getting drunk. Lauren eyeballs the tables of food, the supply of hors d'oeuvres nearly depleted, and she thinks to grab something before her chance is gone, but decides against it. If drunk is what she's going to be, then drunk she will be.

"Robin? Nope," says Ian. "Year after. Same as your—"

She watches him stop himself, watches him realize what he was about to say. Then he ducks his head and shakes it.

"It's okay," she tells him, squeezing his arm.

"No," he says, stuttering. "I'm... I—"

"It's okay, Ian. We've all lost people."

He finally looks at her again, managing a weak smile. "It's just," he says, "it's just that I *just* did the same thing with Michael over there." He nods his head toward the other side of the room. "I mentioned his sister without thinking about it, that is. Only that was probably worse, since she died 2 years ago and not 20."

"Which one is Michael?" asks Lauren.

Ian points him out, and the bearded fellow in the tweed coat is so far removed from the mopey kid who meandered past her house on his paper route that she'd thought him someone's husband on first glance. He's holding court with a couple of guys, telling a story with his hands as much as his mouth, and people on his periphery are starting to get sucked in. The cheerleader and the artist, who'd been getting rather cozy with each other over in the corner, they turn to Michael now too.

"I don't remember him being that charismatic," she says to Ian.

"Well," says Ian. "He's a professor now."

"Of?"

"Art," says Ian. "Out in Hawaii. Tenured and everything."

Ian is saying something else now, but Lauren is focused on the two drink tickets he's been fiddling with since they started talking. Her gaze passes between the tickets and Michael, Michael and the tickets, the tickets and—

I'll be at Elaine's, her mother is repeating in her head now. *If you'd like the house to yourself.*

"Ian," she says, squeezing his arm again. "You going to use those?"

Ian raises an eyebrow, confused.

"Your tickets," says Lauren, taking hold of his wrist, shaking the hand and the tickets playfully in front of his face.

"Oh," says Ian. "No. But haven't you, like, haven't you had enough?"

"Not for what I have in mind," she says, plucking the tickets from his hand and heading for the perky blonde at the drink cart.

"What do you have in mind?" says Ian.

"Drink, sir," she says, patting his cheek, "is a great provoker."

"And what are you hoping it will provoke?"

"Lechery, sir. Lechery."

"But lechery," says Ian, as she collects her drinks, "it provokes and it unprovokes. Remember?"

"For men maybe," she says, downing the first drink in one hard swallow.

"And, besides," says Ian, "lechery with who?"

"Who do you think?" she says, downing the second drink and handing both empty glasses to Ian.

"But I've told you," he seems to be saying. But what he's told her is something she didn't hear before, something she doesn't hear this time either.

THE CROWD HAS THINNED out around him by the time she gets there, so Lauren is free to make whatever move she wants. But she can't decide if he's a hugger, and he has his hands in his pockets besides, so she simply gets close enough that he might hear her through the din, and she leans in to check his name tag (something she's seen countless people do tonight as a way of getting things going).

"Michael," she says. "Michael, Michael, Michael."

"Hey, Lauren," he says with a smile.

She's pretty sure he didn't look to her chest for her name, and she's suddenly sad that, even if he did remember her name, he didn't use the logistics of the event as an excuse to take a free peek. She's also not sure why she said his name four times, and she's about to walk away when he speaks again.

"How you been?" he says.

She puts a hand on his arm as she says, "You're so sweet to ask," and then, feeling just the slightest hint of muscle on an arm where she expected to find none, she adds, "My god, you're hot."

Lauren cannot understand why she's said it, but he laughs, and that seems a good enough reason to say it again. "No, seriously," she says, waving a finger around and nodding in the direction of everyone else. "You're the hottest guy in this room."

Michael looks down, still grinning, but blushing now too.

She draws closer, lowering her voice as she leans in. "No," she says, cupping her hand over his ear. "Seriously. Don't be embarrassed."

"I'm not, Lauren," is what he says, looking at her again, a kind look in his eyes, the kind of look she hopes he will give her when they're back at her place and she's on top of him.

She hopes she has not just said that out loud.

"It's just," he says, but she doesn't let him finish.

"What?" she says. "Are you—are you gay? I thought that was your cousin."

"That was my cousin," he says. "Two of them, actually. Me, I'm—"

She puts a finger to his lips and then holds her free hand to his chest. "The hottest guy in the room," she says. "That's what you are."

"Lauren," he says, "how much have you—?"

"No one's asked me," she says, drawing closer to him, a hand on both arms now and both hands squeezing. "No one's asked me why I'm wearing this dress. No one remembers. No one remembers, Michael. But you—"

"Your brother," he says.

"See!" she says, walking a pair of fingers up his tie, from his chest to his chin, the fingers like the legs of the itsy bitsy spider they imagined when they were kids. "See," she says, "I knew you knew."

Behind her, she suddenly feels a hand on her shoulder—a thick, meaty hand.

"Lauren," says Ian. "Come on."

"What?" says Lauren, shrugging Ian's hand off her shoulder. "I haven't even asked him yet."

"Lauren," says Ian.

"Asked me what?" says Michael.

"If you'll come home with me," says Lauren. "My mother's gone. I have the house to—"

"Lauren," says Ian. "He's married!"

Lauren stares into Michael's eyes, hoping they'll tell her the truth she'd rather hear. But eyes can't speak, she knows. She knows that, even through the fog that's lifting now, lifting faster than it ever has before. She lets go of the arm she still has hold of, pulls her other hand from his face, and stands there before him, waiting to be judged. She looks around her, searching for other judges, other verdicts about her being cast down from on high, but no one else is paying her any attention at all.

"I'm sorry," says Michael.

"Sorry for being married?" says Lauren, hating the still-playful tone in her voice, hating the corner of her lip that twitches ever so slightly upward as she speaks this terrible line, hating too the eyebrow that arches in invitation.

"No," he starts to say, but she cuts him off.

"Because if you're sorry about that," she begins, wishing she would shut up but unable to stop the words from spilling out of her, "if you're sorry about that, the offer still stands."

"Lauren," says Ian, his hand on her shoulder again, now with a firmer grip. "Let me take you home."

"You're married too," she says as she turns on him. She gives him a raspberry, her spit showering his un-expectant face. And then, finally, she storms out.

৵৵৽

HER SHOES IN HAND, she walks in stocking feet through the center of town toward home. It is cold, sobering. She smiles at that thought, at her second great pun of the night, but then she is crying. It isn't until the river of tears and mascara and snot finally trickles into her mouth that she stops. She gags, coughing for a moment, and she stumbles into the shrubbery at the back of the old Quick Mart's parking lot. It's closed now, so there's no one to laugh at her, and that makes the decision to sit so much easier. Sure, she's almost home, but she's not sure that's where she belongs. At least not yet.

Lauren stares for a long time at the back door of the place, trying to remember a story from her high school days. There was a robbery here, she remembers, and the kids jockeying the register claimed someone had attacked them from the bushes during a smoke break. But then it turned out they did the deed themselves, one of them shooting the other so they could make off with the pittance that was in the safe.

At least she thinks that's how it went. She's not sure she trusts her memory right now. Or any other part of herself, for that matter.

A few cars pass, one or two even making the turn on 27 that she was about to make, the turn that would take her home. And suddenly it occurs to her that if Michael wandered by her house delivering papers back in the day, that maybe that meant Michael lived nearby. And that maybe meant that he was staying with his parents while he was home for the reunion. Lauren stands up. She can't sit here. What if he passes by? She tugs at the hemline of her dress, slaps at her ass to brush the dust away, and is just about to get going when she hears foot-steps coming up the hill out of the center. Footsteps and a voice.

"I guess we had the same idea," says Michael before she can get away.

Lauren wipes at her face, trying to clean it up before he can see her properly, but she can feel the make-up smearing as she does, and she realizes it's useless.

He stops a few feet from her and offers a kind smile. "Can I walk you home?" he asks.

All she can manage is a nod.

They walk for a minute without saying anything else at all. Then Michael says, "When my sister died a couple of years ago, I thought of you."

Lauren thinks it an awkward comment, but appreciates his attempt to find common ground. Dead siblings are as good a topic as any for small talk, right?

"I was a mess," he says. "And I thought about how you got through all of senior week—graduation, and the banquet, and prom—"

"I didn't go to prom," says Lauren.

"I know," says Michael. "Or, well, I know now. Ian told me. But I thought you had. That's how strong I thought you were."

"You give me too much credit," says Lauren.

"I looked you up on Facebook once," says Michael, "saw that you looked happy, that you were married—"

"Divorced now," she tells him, correcting him.

He turns and gives her another smile. "And you survived that, too," he says.

A car passes, headed toward the center, its high beams blinding them as it comes round the bend. And so they stop for a moment, shielding their eyes with an arm a piece. When the light is gone, Lauren lowers her arm and sees her house ahead on the corner.

"You inspired me," says Michael. "I guess that's what I'm trying to say."

"Because I'm a survivor?" asks Lauren, stepping ahead, eager to get home so she can get back to crying, now that he's given her tear ducts fresh ammunition.

"Yeah," says Michael. "I figured: if you could get through all of that as a teenager, then through the rest of it as an adult, then maybe I could suck it up and deal too."

They're at the fence that circles her house now, her fingers playing with the latch on the gate.

"I'm sorry," says Michael.

"For being married?" says Lauren.

He chuckles. "No, I'm sorry for rambling. I thought I could make you feel better. With my story, I mean."

"I'm happy to have survived," she says, unlatching the gate and stepping into her yard. "But that's all I've ever done, Michael. That's all I've ever done."

THERE IS snow on the ground when she wakes for her morning run after a few uneasy hours of sleep, but she gets dressed anyway, finds her pedometer on the nightstand amongst empty water bottles and a near-empty bottle of ibuprofen, and then heads downstairs.

Her mother protests, rattles off the list of excuses Lauren has to stay inside this morning, but she plugs her earbuds into her ears, waves goodbye, and gets on her way.

At the spot where her brother died, she does as she usually does and jogs in place long enough to imagine him there in the ditch. But then something changes. She catches a glimpse of what she's left behind her—a trail of sneaker prints in the snow—and she can't bear to look at them. So, this morning she doesn't turn around; she keeps running. Maybe, she thinks, if she's careful, she'll never have to stop.

IRON GRETEL

Once upon a time, when the prince was but a wee lad, he invented a counting game. Locked in the tower by himself, it was left to the boy to conjure his own amusements. And that was how he came to make a sport of betting on the lives of his father's huntsmen.

"How long will this one last?" the prince asked himself each time. "And what about this one? How long will *he* live before the trees make him their supper?"

Many a moon passed before the king grew tired of the howls issuing from deep within his woods. Many a moon passed, and many a hunter, but the prince never tired of watching the trees close in. He liked to guess how many birds would flee from the uppermost branches as oak and fir leaned in for the kill, as birch and elm made ready to strip flesh from bone.

Later, when he decided it wasn't the trees themselves doing the killing, the prince liked to imagine what manner of beast it might be that called the forest home. What creature could so easily devour the strapping young men who presented themselves to his father—their teeth gleaming, their chins chiseled, their hair cropped impossibly close to their heads in what was then the style? The huntsmen seemed invincible to the prince, even from his high perch in the tower, even at that distance. What could best them? What in the world?

After one final try to make safe the forest, the last seven of his majesty's hunters embarking on the quest together and never returning, the king decreed that the woods were unsafe and off limits to all. The prince watched the proclamation from the tower, counting the wrinkles on his father's forehead, watching as the old man rubbed the back of his neck on the way down from the dais. All pretense of bravery and assuredness had gone from his weary countenance. There were three more wrinkles than the last time the prince had seen the king.

Years passed. The prince reached the precipice of manhood, his voice crackling and straining as his body stretched uncomfortably taller. He was reminded of an old tale his mother used to read to him by his bedside in the tower, the story of wing-makers, a father and son who flew too close to heaven and were struck down for their impertinence. The prince began to slump his shoulders forward, the way his father now did. Perhaps if he feigned the plight of the old, God could be tricked into sparing him their fate.

It was on the eve of his thirteenth birthday, the day he would be released from the tower, that the prince spied a most peculiar sight. Through the courtyard came a hooded figure. The figure carried a crossbow, a sword, and a heavy satchel. A hunter, thought the prince. The first to arrive in their starving, cursed country in ages. And yet, that was not what made the sight peculiar. The strangeness of the scene was made plain only when the hood of the figure was lowered to reveal not a man, but a woman.

The prince, for the first time, felt a stirring in his loins. She was a pretty thing, now that the hood was down. Hair the color of copper, skin the color of milk—and, he now noticed, a goodly bosom beneath her cloak and tunic.

She shouted for the king or his representative, and the old

man trudged out from the palace gates to meet her, leaning heavily upon his scepter.

They spoke in hushed tones, so that the prince could not make out the purpose of their intercourse no matter how hard he strained, no matter how far through the window he leaned.

But then, then the king raised a weary arm toward the forest. Weary, yet welcoming. The huntress bowed to him and made her way into the woods.

And the prince began to count.

When he reached one hundred and still she did not scream, the stirring in his loins became a full-on discomfort. He reached into his breeches to adjust himself and recoiled in horror at the tiny drop of moisture he found there. He breathed easier when, upon inspection, he saw that it was not blood.

And then he refocused. He stared out at the treetops, waiting. But they did not close in as they always had before. His curiosity was swelling.

When that night his mother came to read to him and serve his evening meal, he begged her to set him free then and there. "I will be a man in mere hours," he said. "Why should I be asleep in this prison when the clock strikes twelve?"

"But what will you do in the dark?" she asked him. "What will you do?"

"I will rescue the huntress," he said. "It is what a prince should do. A man!"

And his mother, weary herself of years spent protecting the boy and serving the king, she sighed and she let him go.

The prince ran towards the forest, stopping only at the blacksmith to demand a sword he did not yet know how to wield. And then, into the woods he went. He focused his gaze on the footprints before him, the bootprints of the huntress, and he followed them.

After a good, long walk, the moon rising in the sky above him, the prince caught sight of a roaring fire in a clearing up ahead.

He drew closer, creeping from the shadows of one tree to another until he could see who sat by the light and warmth of the fire. She was drinking from a flask and smiling, her foot toying with something long and metal—her sword, he suddenly realized —which was planted in between the shoulder blades of a man covered in white-blonde hair from his head to his feet.

The prince's foot crushed a fallen branch then, as he stepped back in amazement, and the crack echoed through the clearing.

The huntress stood in a flash, her crossbow aimed right at him.

"You," she called out. "You there in the shadows, come into the light."

The prince did as he was told.

"You are the prince," the huntress said with a smile.

"I am," he said.

"If you will but lower your sword," she said, lowering her own weapon, "I will give you the bow you are owed."

"Oh," said the prince, not realizing that he still held the sword. He dropped it.

The huntress bowed, then said, "Will you join me?"

The prince stayed put. He asked, "Who is it you've killed?"

The huntress smiled again. "The monster what dwelled here," she said, pointing to a small pond the prince could only now make out, now that his eyes had begun to adjust to the light.

"But he," the prince stammered, "he killed all those men."

"Indeed he did," said the huntress. "Please," she said. "Join me, your highness. It's a lot warmer over here."

The prince took a few steps toward her. "But how did you—?" he said, trailing off, hoping she would finish his sentence for him.

She nudged the hilt of her sword with her foot. "With that," she said.

"But you," said the prince. "You're a... a woman."

The huntress laughed, her chortle filling the clearing with a glee that sent the prince back a step, then two.

"I surely am," she said. "And if you come closer, I'll prove it to you. Manhood is upon you," she said. "Is it not?"

The prince said nothing as she did what she did next—as she stood and ambled toward him, unlacing her tunic as she drew nearer. When she was too close for comfort, when he could see that her green eyes were flecked with gold, he stared over her shoulder at the beast he'd long imagined. The body was so small. Muscled, yes. Hairy as a beast should be. But small.

The huntress draped her arms over the prince's shoulders. "Are you ready?" she asked.

"No," the prince cried out as he ducked out from under her embrace. "No," he cried as he raced back toward the palace, the huntress' laughter following him through the woods like a pack of dogs nipping at his heels, never seeming to grow fainter no matter how much distance he put between himself and her.

"No," he said to his mother, as she ran her fingers through his disheveled hair, as she dried his tears with the sheet of his bed in the tower. "No," he said. "I am not ready."

HARD TO FIND

E ddie stood in front of his comic book store, his trench coat scarfed about him, and watched through the big picture window as Ashley rung up her last customer. The boy she was waiting on stood eye-level with her chest and was grinning ear to ear as she, seemingly oblivious—but not oblivious at all, Eddie knew, not at all—counted out his change. Outside, Eddie found himself grinning too.

This was why he employed only girls to run his register. Selling comics was about selling fantasy, and not just the fantasy of the comics themselves, but the fantasy that at least part of that fantasy wasn't really a fantasy at all. A hot girl behind the counter of the local funny book shop? And one who let you stare at her tits without a reprimand? That wasn't supposed to happen in real life. And yet, here she was.

Eddie slipped into the shop as the customer slipped out, and he gave Ashley a nod in greeting as he stepped behind the counter to join her. Then he started in on emptying his pockets. First came his wallet—empty now, except for a maxed-out MasterCard, an expired Massachusetts driver's license, and a half dozen receipts. Next came his worn spiral-bound notebook, the one meant for figuring the store's finances, but which had become his doodle pad. And then, finally, came a broken padlock.

"All gone, huh?"

"I don't know," said Eddie. "Probably. I didn't bother to hoist the door once I saw the lock."

Ashley nodded, then crouched down to retrieve something from the small fridge they kept behind the counter.

"You get my dinner?" asked Eddie.

Ashley nodded again, setting in front of him a chilled bottle of chocolate milk and an eighty-nine cent package of Hostess Donettes.

"Thanks," said Eddie.

"You know," said Ashley, "you could splurge once in a while. This hunger strike you've been on since she left—"

"Not really a hunger strike," said Eddie, cutting her off as he popped one of the miniature donuts into his mouth.

"Well, whatever this is," said Ashley, "it needs to stop. You've got the money to treat yourself better."

Eddie shook his head, then reached into the inside pocket of his coat. He set the folded letter down in front of her, nodded at her to read it, and then waited.

When she was finished, she looked up at him with weary eyes, eyes sadder than her eighteen years entitled her to. "How?" said Ashley. "Are you really that far behind?"

Eddie nodded.

"But we do better business than Hot Comix and Greg's combined," she said. "What the hell am I doing wearing this low-cut shit all the time if not to keep the store in the black?"

Eddie shrugged, then stepped away from her. At the window, he stood and watched the traffic backing up along Alpine Lane, cars waiting to turn left or right to join the hustle and bustle of the main drag. The automobiles speeding along Chelmsford Street seemed united against those lined up on Alpine, and Eddie enjoyed watching soccer moms stuck in front of his store growing aggravated. He watched them clutch their steering wheels tighter, watched the swears form on their lips as they looked to their backseats to make sure their children were asleep. They cursed the town that would not install a traffic light here, despite this little side street being home to not only the post office but the best bakery around. But Eddie, he loved it when cars jammed up right outside his door. It's why he did better business than the guys across the street: if traffic was backed up bad enough, kids dragged along with their moms on errands needed only to peer out to the right, point at the sign for The Splash Page, and say, "Mom! Please?!?"

Behind him, Ashley was apologizing about something as she gathered up her things.

"Don't worry about it," said Eddie.

"Somebody's got to worry about it," said Ashley.

Eddie turned around to face her. "That somebody ain't you," he said. "At least not anymore. You and your chest have done your duty for king and country. And now you're free to peddle your wares—"

"And to wear only petals," she said.

He snorted back a laugh. "That's right," he said. "Over at Mac's, the guys'll be lining up for *you* now, not Superman. And you'll finally be getting the money that you deserve."

"You've always paid me what I—"

He set a hand on her shoulder and she stopped talking. "It ain't your problem, Ash. Okay?"

But she said nothing. Instead, she reached up with her own hand and squeezed his.

They stood in silence for a moment before Ashley asked "What's happening to the money?" She ran her free hand along the top of the glass display cases that formed their counter. "You've sold so many of the big ticket books. You should be all set," she said. "I mean, that's part of why I'm leaving. I thought you were all set."

"I'll be fine," said Eddie.

Ashley held up the letter he'd given her.

He stalked away from her like it was kryptonite.

"You're being evicted," she said. "You are *not* going to be fine. Where are you going to go? I mean, this isn't just your shop now." She pointed to the table of long boxes which occupied the center of the store, to the skirt of the burlap tablecloth. "You've been sleeping under the Goddamn table too, ever since Alice went back to her dad's."

Eddie grabbed Ashley's leather jacket from the coat stand and tossed it at her. Then he said, "Don't worry about me, kid."

"Fine," she said, putting on the jacket. But just as soon as she'd put it on, she was taking it off again.

"What?" said Eddie.

Ashley pointed over his shoulder toward the window. "The Talker," she said. "He's coming."

Eddie turned around and squinted. Then he sighed. Sure enough, there was the old bastard now, making his way past Skip's Restaurant, his unmistakable orange wool cap bobbing up and down as he waddled this way.

༺༻

IF YOU'D EVER JOCKEYED a grocery store register in Chelmsford, you feared the Talker. It didn't matter if you worked the Market Basket on the Lowell line, the Shop and Save over on Drum Hill, or the Purity Supreme in the center of town—this codger got around. The best you could hope for when he came into your store was that he picked someone else's register, not yours. Otherwise, you were shit out of luck.

Eddie had thought he was done with the old fool when he opened his own place, a place where food wasn't sold at all. But the Talker, it seemed, liked comic books too.

A typical conversation with him wasn't a conversation at all; it was a monologue, and it went something like this: "What, uh, what, what, what grade are you in there? Do you, did that—did that ring up properly? Are you sure that's the right price? Oh, uhm, OK. Uh, here you go. Here you go." He'd dig into his pockets and hand you a crumpled up wad of ones and fives, quarters and dimes. And then, before you had a chance to say anything, he'd continue. "That's the money," he'd say, pointing. "That's the money for my order there. Is that enough? Is it enough? I have more if you need it," he'd say, gesturing toward his socks.

A couple of years ago, the Talker happened upon Alice's register at the Market Basket. It was before the comic book store, before the wedding, before the evening in her father's basement that made the wedding a necessity. Back then, Eddie was just the bag boy checking *her* out while she checked out the customers. Just a kid who should've been in college (but wasn't), admiring the ass of a high school girl in a mini skirt. Inspecting her merchandise while she passed produce back to him to pack absentmindedly into plastic bags.

"I'd like paper inside the plastic," the Talker told him. "You know how to do that, right? Do you need to call someone to show you? I can ask the manager, if you like."

Alice smiled at Eddie as she slid a box of Little Debbie Zebra Cakes over the scanner and down onto the conveyor belt.

Eddie smiled back at her and said nothing to the Talker, who went back to watching prices ring up on the tiny LCD screen above the register. "Do you," the Talker began again, "do you, do you know which way it is to East Chelmsford? My cousin's over that way. I need to get there. Do you know the way? Which way is it to East Chelmsford? You know the way, don't you?"

Alice turned to Eddie as she rang up the last item, a two liter of Coca Cola Classic. "You know which way that is, Eddie?"

Eddie turned to the Talker and said, "No hablo ingles, señor."

Eddie watched Alice try to hold back a smile as she totaled up the Talker's order, as the Talker told her, "He should speak English. You should get him some lessons. They teach English over at the university. Do you know Spanish? You should tell him that. Tell him to take some lessons. You should—"

Alice cut him off then. "That'll be four dollars and ninety-five cents, sir."

And that was where it had all begun for Eddie and her, in the suppressed laughter they shared that afternoon, in the commiserating they did on their lunch break later on, and after the movie he took her to that night, at the Route 3 Cinema across the street. That was where it began. Eddie supposed he should be thankful to the old bastard, but Eddie never did the things he should have done.

⚜

THE TALKER TODDLED into The Splash Page, and for once he said nothing. He ignored Eddie and Ashley and went straight for the racks on the far end of the store. He plucked the latest issue of *The New Warriors* off of the shelf and began to read it.

"Crisis averted," said Ashley.

"For now," said Eddie. "When he's done, he'll—"

Ashley tapped at her wristwatch, cutting him off. "You're almost closed. Let him read till then, then shoo him out."

"You make it sound so simple," said Eddie.

"Yeah," said Ashley, sighing. "Bad habit of mine."

Eddie grabbed his notebook and began to doodle.

"You know," whispered Ashley, "if she'd kept it, it might have ended up like him."

"Kept what?" asked Eddie, not looking up from his drawing.

"She told me the technician found all sorts of anomalies during the exam."

Eddie continued to sketch. "What are we talking about?"

"You know damn well what I'm talking about," she said. "And you know damn well what I'm trying to say."

Eddie put his pen down and looked at her. "I'm not sure I do," he said.

"She had no choice!" said Ashley, raising her voice now.

"No choice?"

Ashley shook her head at him. "There are five stages of grief, Eddie. And she'd come back if only you'd get past the first."

"And the first is?"

Ashley slipped her jacket on again. "The first," she said, "is not just a river in Egypt."

Eddie snorted back a laugh. Then he composed himself and went back to his drawing. It was only as Ashley made her way toward the door that he spoke. "You know," he said. "You're wrong."

"About what?"

On the other side of the store, the Talker giggled at the book he was reading. Eddie stared at the back of the old man's orange hat as he spoke, imagining a smaller version of it on a smaller head.

"Even if I did stop denying whatever it is that I'm supposedly denying," said Eddie, "she still wouldn't come back. You don't know her like I—"

"That's bullshit," said Ashley.

The Talker coughed and then, under his breath, without looking away from his comic book, mumbled, "Language, language, language."

Ashley returned to Eddie's side. "You think I haven't seen the tears?" she said. "I've seen what she'll suffer to be with you."

"What about what I suffer to be with her?" he said. "What about that?"

Ashley stared at him for a moment, and he stared back, trying to see what she was trying to see. But then came the shock and the pain of her slap, the sting. He closed his eyes and focused on the throbbing of his cheek. And that was how he never saw Ashley leave. He barely even heard her go, the closing of the door behind her so unlike the slam he expected that she might simply have vanished through the door without opening it at all.

"Tsk, tsk," said the Talker. "A kiss can be a comma, a question mark, or an exclamation point. But a slap is a period, always a period, always the end. The end, the end, the..."

Eddie opened his eyes as the old man trailed off, waiting for what would come next.

"And in the end," the Talker warbled. "The love you take—"

"You shouldn't come in here anymore," said Eddie, cutting him off.

The Talker looked at Eddie, blinked twice, and then went back to his reading.

"Did you hear me, old man?" Eddie shouted. "I don't want you in here."

Eddie waited, but the Talker did not talk.

"Don't you live somewhere?" said Eddie. "East Chelmsford, right? That's where you're always headed, right?"

The mere mention of that place made the Talker pause. He closed the book he was reading and set it atop the table of long boxes. "My, uh, cousin's over that way," he began. "Do you know the way? I thought you only spoke Spanish. You listened to my advice, didn't you? You remember when I gave you advice? Back when you worked at the grocery store? You remember that, don't you? I said you should speak English. Which store was that?"

"If your cousin's in East Chelmsford," said Eddie. "Why are you always asking for directions? Shouldn't you know your way by now?"

"I forgot," said the Talker. "I forgot. I, uh..." He shook his head from side to side, first with a gentle sway, then with more violent force. He swayed backward and forward, trembling all over. But then he picked up his comic again and flipped it back open and his hands shook less.

Eddie looked up at the Super Friends wall clock. "We close in five minutes," he told the Talker. He stared at the old man, waiting for some sign of recognition, but none came.

Instead, the Talker began to talk again. "What happened to your wife?" he asked. "Did you hit her?"

"We argued," said Eddie. "But I never hit her, no."

"It's wrong to hit a woman," said the Talker. "You know that, don't you? You're a good man, Charlie Brown. I can tell." The Talker paused, looked over at Eddie. "What were you fighting about? What was it you were fighting about?"

"None of your business."

"That's the thing people say to me the most," he said. "When they say anything at all. People don't usually talk to me, you see. People usually don't say a word."

Eddie scoffed, "Maybe that's because you never stop talking yourself."

The old man waddled across the store. As he drew closer, Eddie thought to pinch his nose, so potent was the pungent stench of dirty laundry and unwashed armpits. But he dared not do anything that would invite further conversation. The Talker tapped his finger on the glass display case, pointing at the last book left within it.

"What?" said Eddie. "You wanna read it?"

The Talker nodded.

"It's not for browsing," said Eddie. "That book's from 1962."

"Sometimes the girls let me look at it. When you're not here."

Eddie inhaled slowly, deeply, trying to calm himself down after that news. But he held it in for longer than he should have, and it hurt when he opened his mouth and let it all out. "If you've got the money, honey," said Eddie, "they've got your disease."

"Oh, they never charged me. No, sir."

Eddie nodded. "Must've thought you were cute."

"My cousin had that book," said the Talker, ignoring Eddie's last words. "He called me on the phone the day he got it, told me

E. CHRISTOPHER CLARK

how wonderful it was. He got on his bike to come show it to me, all the way from East Chelmsford, and he was reading it again while he rode. That's when the car hit him."

"The what?" said Eddie.

"He's dead now," said the Talker. "Roadkill. Like a skunk, only he didn't stink as much."

"I..." Eddie stuttered. "That's..."

The Talker tapped on the glass again. "May I see it now? May I see it?"

Eddie stared at the Talker, wanting the old man to look at him, hoping for some sign in that wrinkled face that would tell him if this was a good idea or not. But the Talker did not look at him. Eddie looked at the old man's hands, his fingers. They were cleaner than he'd expected, but there was still dirt under the fingernails. Under each and every one, except for the thumbs. *Did the old man still suck his thumbs?* Eddie wondered. He was a child in so many ways, after all. It was a stomach-churning thought, that thumb in that mouth, that tongue digging underneath that fingernail.

But then his stomach stopped churning, and a single sentence from a green pamphlet scrolled across the big screen of his mind like a piece of breaking news: *Thumbsucking has been documented at 7 weeks from concepti—*

Eddie squeezed his eyes shut to stop this, but it didn't help.

"Are you crying?" asked the Talker. "Are you crying, Charlie Brown? Did Lucy take the football away again?"

Thumbsucking has been documented—

"My cousin used to clip Charlie Brown out of the paper. Kept them all in a cigar box we stole from our fathers. Poor, old Charlie Brown. You never got to kick the football."

Thumbsucking—

"SHUT UP!" said Eddie, slamming his fists down upon the countertop, glass shattering as he did.

The Talker shook his head as he backed away. "They should

have let you kick the football. They should have. Just once. Even just once," he said.

Eddie cleared the glass off of the book the old man had been pointing at and handed it to him. "Take this," said Eddie. "Take it and don't ever come back."

"I..." the Talker stuttered. "I don't have it. I don't have the money to pay you. Maybe if I get out to East Chelmsford, I can ask my cousin for a loan. I spent all my allowance on Hershey bars today. Will you save it for me? Will you save—"

"I don't want your money," said Eddie, forcing the book into the Talker's hands. "I just want you to leave."

The Talker looked down at the comic book, rubbed his thumbs over its polypropylene sleeve. Then he looked at Eddie, gave him a nod, and waddled off.

Once the old man was gone, Eddie filled his pockets. He grabbed the lock, the wallet, and what was left of his dinner. He grabbed the keys. And then he opened the register. From beneath the cash drawer, he took the bank book he'd labeled "College fund." And then, setting the drawer back in place, he flipped up the plastic weight that held the twenties down and slipped a folded photograph out from underneath the small stack of bills. He unfolded the sonogram and stared at it.

"Where are you?" Eddie asked the photograph of his lost love's womb, searching its murky lines for that pea-sized something he'd never been able to find on his own. "Where are you?" he asked again. "Where did you go?"

GOOD GRIEF

I t's a strange place for a farm, Charles thinks, smooshed between a highway off-ramp and a strip mall, but a text from Lu assures him that this is the place. So, he flips on the car's blinker and prepares to make the turn.

While he waits for the light to change, Charles adjusts his rearview to check in on the old dog in the backseat. He appears to be asleep, his head resting on the keys of the typewriter that Lu used to lure him inside. Charles wonders if it's the same one the dog kept in his red house back in the day. Then he wonders if the goggles, helmet, and scarf his little sister used to dress the dog up in—Charles wonders if those might have worked as bait too.

The honk of a car's horn breaks him from his reverie. "Wake up, you bald asshole!" someone shouts.

❧

THE FARM IS no ordinary farm. It's a shelter for unwanted animals. In the front there are barns for horses and livestock; further away from the road, there's a building for more common pets. And it's under the

sloped roof of that well-appointed and air conditioned structure that
Charles explains his situation to a woman named Doolittle. Charles
is unsure how to address her. There are diplomas on the wall, several
of them—including a doctorate—but he thinks they may belong to a
parent; she looks far too young to be so accomplished.

"Mister Br—" she begins, once he's finished his explanation.

"Please," he interrupts, "call me—"

"Chuck," she says with a smile.

"Actually," he says, "only my ex ever calls me that."

"Your ex? I thought you said you were married."

"My first wife," he says by way of clarification. "It didn't last
long. Just a phase," he says, "before she and the woman she's
married to now finally realized that they were, you know..."

"Well," says Doolittle. "Charlie then. You don't look like a
Charles to me."

"Charlie is fine," says Charles.

Doolittle smiles again. She's got a piece of lettuce stuck
between her teeth, or maybe kale, but Charles doesn't know how
to tell her without coming across like a blockhead.

"So," says Charles, "can you help me?"

"Just so we're clear," says Doolittle, "you want to trade in your
dog? That very good boy that you—"

"I don't want to," says Charles. "But my wife—"

Doolittle nods. "I understand," she says.

"But it has to be a trade," says Charles. "That is, I need a new
pet. A comfort animal of some sort. My therapist says I absolutely
must have one. My new therapist that is. Not my wife. She had to
stop being my therapist once we were engaged, of course.
Though, of course, if you ask me, those two are in cahoots. My
wife and my therapist, I mean."

"Did you have anything in mind?"

"Well no," says Charles. "As I said, I don't really want to give
up my dog. He's been in the family for years. I've had him since I

was a kid. But Lu, she never liked him. Not even back then when we were in grade school together."

Doolittle shuffles through a stack of paper on her desk, mumbling to herself in between shakes of her head. There are a few minutes of silence between them as she searches for whatever it is she's looking for. And then, it's as if he can see a lightbulb go on above her head.

"I think I have just the thing," says Doolittle.

❦

IN ONE OF the barns out front, with broken down nags neighing and defecating all around him, Charles stares down into the depths of a stall he at first took to be empty. Inside, trudging back and forth atop a bed of thistle, is a runt of a donkey with a missing tail.

"I thought you said he was gray," says Charles. "He looks a little blue to me."

"Well, Charlie, aren't we all a little blue in this day and age? Given the state of the world, I mean."

Doolittle laughs at her own joke. Mercifully, the guffaw dislodges the leafy detritus that was, he realizes with a turn of his stomach, still caught between her teeth.

Doolittle collects herself. "More purple than blue," she says. "No?"

Charles squints. "Perhaps," he says. "I suppose it depends on the light."

"Now," says Doolittle. "Looks can be deceiving, Charlie. So you should know that this lovely boy comes to us from the estate of a wealthy British gentleman who doted upon this fellow and the rest of his menagerie until the day he passed."

"He kept other animals?" asks Charles, a bit more hope in his voice than he intended. After all, it isn't as if the donkey is a terrible animal. Or a terrible idea for a pet. Maybe, like the

Christmas trees he favors, this guy just needs a little love. A home.

"The other animals?" says Doolittle. "I'm afraid they've all been taken. It was quite the collection, though. A bear, a pig, a pair of kangaroos—"

"He seems quiet enough," says Charles, crouching down to look the animal in the eyes. "Quieter than my dog, at the very least. Lu will appreciate that."

The donkey makes its way across the stall to the gate and peers through a gap between the slats at Charles. He seems to frown, the donkey, as he sizes up the tired old fool on the other side of the gate. Then the donkey gives a perfunctory little nod, as if to say "Oh well," as if to say, "You'll do." It reminds Charles of the way his dog would stare him down, now and again, when he refused to play the jazz record that the beagle favored as its soundtrack for raising a ruckus. The donkey and the dog—both of them seemed to know who was in charge, and they knew it wasn't Charles.

Charles sighs. He isn't sure this is the right thing, isn't sure if maybe he should ask to see something in the way of a cat instead —maybe some hefty ball of fur that will do little but sleep on his lap and lap at the last of his lasagna on Thursday nights. He isn't sure of anything at all. But then his phone buzzes in his pocket, and he knows without looking that it's Lu wondering what's taking him so long, and that she won't stop texting until he gives her an answer. So, Charles looks at Doolittle and says, "Good grief, let's get this over with."

THE CARCASS OF THE GHOST

It was only a matter of time before Franny had to kill her brother. They sat in her car, in a parking lot off the Daniel Webster Highway. And while he stared at the door to the record store, her gaze was fixed on the glove compartment. That was where she'd hidden the gun she'd bought at a Salem pawn shop while he watched the horses race at Rockingham Park. That was where her ticket to the future lay, the key to unshackle her from the chains of their past. She closed her eyes and prayed that they would leave soon, that they would get on with the third and final act of the third-rate production they called their life.

"Maybe she isn't coming," she told her brother.

He said nothing, had nothing to say.

"Are you sure it was ten years?" she asked. "Not fifteen? Not twenty?"

He fiddled with the cracked CD case in his hands, opened and closed the lid of it. Under his breath, he mumbled something that sounded vaguely like "She promised."

"Promised what?" said Franny. "Promised a fifteen year old boy that, in ten years, they'd see who chose the better bootleg?"

Franny's brother grunted.

"Don't you think you're taking the whole thing a tad too literally?"

He grunted again, then laid his head on the dash. His fingers played with the latch on the glove compartment.

"Let's go home," said Franny.

Her brother sat up straight and stared her down. His eyes were already dead. She wished she could have shot the poor wretch right there, put him out of his misery. "Don't you remember that night?" he said. "Don't you remember? You were right there. It wasn't... I'm not—"

She placed two fingers on his lips to quiet him. She remembered all too well, try as she had to forget. "She isn't coming," said Franny. But in the silence that followed her proclamation came the sign he'd been waiting for, the proof that she was wrong.

The car shook at the deafening pop of an exhaust system backfiring behind them. Franny's brother whipped his head around to see who had come, but he already knew. Franny could see in his eyes, in the split second before he turned, that he knew. And then, there it was, the specter of the past that should not have been: a purple Harley with a green flame job and a misfit couple sitting astride it. And, as if she needed to provide further proof, the woman on the bike pulled a CD case from her pocket.

"It's them," shouted Franny's brother, slapping his sister on the shoulder. "It's her."

The bike tore off out of the parking lot and through the next one over, the only way to head north.

"C'mon!"

Franny thought of protesting, thought of telling him that they didn't need to do this, but she knew that was a lie, and even as she thought this she was putting the car into gear.

Franny followed the bike up the D.W., the lights staying or turning green all along the route, as if the god of traffic, that usually spiteful sprite, was trying to speed them on their way. And, as she followed it, a small part of her brain could not help but drift backwards in time. Ten years ago, in this same car, Franny had sat in that same parking lot, waiting for her brother to emerge. The only difference then was the record store itself. Back in the day, it had been a hole-in-the-wall indie, known for its bootlegs above all else. Now it was just another link in a failing regional chain.

Ten years ago, she had watched them emerge from the shop, her brother and a girl that Franny did not know. Franny had watched them argue—it was playful, but it was still an argument —and then she had watched that same bike whisk the girl away, the girl's arms wrapped around the waist of someone who was not Franny's crestfallen brother. "Ten years," her brother had told her, as he slipped back into the car. "Ten years," he said. "We'll see."

A hand on her shoulder brought her back to the here and now. "The turnpike," said her brother. "They're getting onto the turnpike."

This had happened before, too. Franny remembered all too well the race up the Everett Turnpike, the way they sped through the New Hampshire night until lurching to a stop at the toll plaza in Merrimack, where there was no change to be found in their car. She remembered how her brother had cursed as the bike disappeared around the bend, how the booth attendant had chided him for doing so, and how they'd searched until dawn for that motorcycle and the pair that had fled on top of it.

Franny and her brother were driving down the same dirt road now, but the bike had not lost them this time. No. Franny shot a glance at her brother. His eyes were screwed up in concentration —his gaze fixed, as ever, on the bike.

"Why does it look like there's only one of them on the bike now?" he asked.

Franny squinted and leaned forward a bit, resting her chin on the steering wheel for a moment. "I have no idea," she told her brother.

"Wait," said her brother. "Now there's nobody. Now there's..."

But what he meant to say never came, for the bike had vanished from the road as if by the will or the wand of some wizard lurking in the pines around them. They drove on, her brother in stunned silence.

When they came to the driveway where they had come before, their headlights shone bright on the same decrepit colonial that had been their final destination all those years ago. Heaps of rusted ornaments littered the lawn on either side of the long driveway, a half-dozen for each season and holiday. And then Franny and her brother saw it. Set amidst that refuse, laid bare on its side, was what had to be a facsimile of the motorcycle they had just chased. It could not be the same one, Franny's brother told her. There were no tires on it, for Christ's sake. The headlamp was broken. And there was gash across the seat, stuffing bleeding out of it.

Franny parked the car, but she kept it running. And, as her brother unbuckled himself to get out, she gave him his last chance. "Let's go home," she said.

But he ignored her, as she knew he would, as she knew he must.

Franny watched him pace through the light of her car's high beams, unable to even approach the carcass of the ghost they had just chased. He was crying out there as she opened the glove compartment, as she checked that the gun was still loaded.

She looked away from him, staring instead at the darkened windows of the house. Franny had not known for sure what happened in there on that night, as the rising sun was changing black sky to blue. She had not known exactly what her brother and the other man had done with the girl inside those walls. But years later, when Franny screamed like she'd heard that girl scream, she knew that it was not a trick of the ears, as her brother had claimed. Franny knew that what happened in that house was not a game. Or, if it was, it was rigged—as all games between boys and girls have been and always will be.

Her brother jumped at the sound of her door opening. "Christ," he said, "You scared me."

She made no secret of the gun in her hand as she rounded the car and stood before him. But he didn't notice it. His head was still turned toward the corpse of the motorcycle. "What's up?" he said.

"Do you remember?" said Franny. "Or is it all a blur?"

"I remember that we came here," he said. "I remember that I went in when she curled a finger in my direction, when she beckoned me to follow. I remember a beer or two. But," he said. "After that... After that, it's a blur."

"I remember," said Franny, raising the gun. "I won't ever forget."

"Franny," he said, his head still turned from her, his eyes still not seeing. "I swear. I may not remember much, but I know it wasn't what you imagined."

It sounded like he was trying to convince himself now. "It was just a game," he said. "Just a—"

She pulled the trigger and shut him up for the last time. And as his body collapsed to the ground, she fired four more times, punctuating each blast with a single word. "No," she said. "It! Was! Not!"

Up in the house, a single window now came aglow. Franny looked up at it as someone peeked through the curtains. The girl stood in the window, pushing her hair out of her eyes and nodding at Franny. Franny nodded back.

Just before she backed out of the driveway, Franny saw the girl descending the front steps with a shovel in hand.

"Next week," the girl shouted, "we do yours."

Franny nodded. Then, before she drove away, she looked at her brother's body one last time. The words "Goodbye, John" were ready on her tongue, but they never made it past her lips.

TOO MUCH FABRIC, TOO MUCH COLOR

He sits on the edge of his daughter's bed and stares out the window at the distant pond where he used to skinny-dip with her mother. Oh, the fun they used to have. Down there. Up here. Up here, in this very room, back when it was his.

With his big toe, he traces the contour of a deep knot in the old hardwood floor. Pam scratched her ass up on this very spot, once upon a time. What a fucking mess. She bled so much that, when they were done, he accused her of being on the rag without telling him. Truth be told, she told him, she hadn't even noticed the wound until the end. He'd been hitting the spot so good, it was like the whole damned world had disappeared.

His other foot catches on something as he slides it absent-mindedly across the floor, and he stops what he's doing to see what he's found. He pinches the piece of fabric between his toes and hoists it upward, his knee and hip creaking in protest at his middle-aged attempt at flexibility.

It's a bikini bottom, he sees now. He runs his fingers along the synthetic fabric, dust flaking off of the forgotten thing, and he wonders whether it belongs to Alice. *Belonged*, he corrects himself, now that he's kicked her out and she's left it behind. It's his now, he supposes, like every other scrap in his now empty nest. But whose *was* it? Old Occam would say it was Alice's for sure—all things being equal, the simplest solution is the right one—but Alice had so many girlfriends up here over the years. It could just as easily have belonged to one of them.

Truth is, this was probably too much fabric for his daughter. This, right here, was more Ashley's style. *Ashley.* Just the thought of her name makes him smile, the sweetness of that *ee* sound at the end—the sweetness Pam denied their daughter, their sharp, sibilant Alice. *Ashley.* Cute brunette. A firecracker with her friends, but always sweet to him.

He remembered how Ashley sat with him that one time last year, waiting for Alice to come home from a night out with Eddie. It was just after Pam left him for good. They sat at the bar in the kitchen, he and Ashley, eating sugar-free Jello out of the little single-serving cups that Alice lived on during the summers. They sat there and they talked about the Sox, and she pretended not to notice him checking her out—never called him out as the dirty old man that he most certainly was.

Alice told him that Ashley strips down at the club in Billerica now, now that she's 18. That makes part of him sad, the part that thinks Ashley could've done anything with her life—anything she wanted. But then there's the part of him that feels certain she's doing *exactly* what she wants to do, that Ashley is the kind of girl who always has and always will.

He takes the bikini bottom with him as he leaves Alice's room, not sure if he is audacious enough to do with it what he is imagining doing with it. The computer in his den is still on, his web browser still opened to the same site. With just enough hesitation to make himself feel better about himself, he heads that way. He clutches the fabric in his fist, trying to remember which color it was that Alice wore all the time, and which color was Ashley's. As he steps into the den, locking the door behind him, he hopes—*prays*—that Alice's color was not purple.

ACKNOWLEDGEMENTS

"The Pieces" was first published in 2010 in *Device* as part of their "Chasing Porcelain" exquisite corpse project.

"Time's Fool" was first published in 2018 in *Commonthought*.

"Iron Gretel" was first performed in 2015 as part of *Five Minute Fairy Tales* at the Seacoast Repertory Theatre in Portsmouth, New Hampshire.

"Hard to Find" was first published in 2012 in *River Muse: Tales of Lowell & the Merrimack Valley*.

"The Carcass of the Ghost" was first published in 2011 in *Commonthought*.

"Too Much Fabric, Too Much Color" was first published in 2010 in *Device* as part of their "She Was Gelatin" exquisite corpse project.

ABOUT THE AUTHOR

E. Christopher Clark is the author of the Stains of Time series, a family saga with a hint of magical realism and a whole lot of time travel. His other books include the short story collections *Out of the Woods* and *Under the World*, the novella *The Seven Wives of Silver*, and a collection of poems cheekily titled *Bad Poetry Night*. His short stories have been published in *Live Free or Ride: Tales of the Concord Coach*, *River Muse: Tales of Lowell & the Merrimack Valley*, and the University of Hawaii's *Vice-Versa*. A graduate of Lesley University's MFA in Creative Writing program, he lives in Massachusetts with his wife and daughters.

echristopherclark.com

facebook.com/eccbooks

x.com/eccbooks

instagram.com/eccbooks

goodreads.com/eccbooks

pinterest.com/eccbooks

amazon.com/E.-Christopher-Clark/e/B00H0G94T0

www.ingramcontent.com/pod-product-compliance
Lightning Source LLC
Chambersburg PA
CBHW021937170626
46807CB00007B/3163